Pete ^{the} Cat

Three Bite Rule

HarperFestival is an imprint of HarperCollins Publishers.

Pete the Cat: Three Bite Rule
Copyright © 2018 by Amazon Content Services LLC /PTC Productions, LLC
Pete the Cat © 1999, 2010 James Dean
Pete the Cat is a registered trademark of Pete the Cat, LLC, US Reg.
#3820216, #4903976, #5104976, #5118017.
www.harpercollinschildrens.com
ISBN 978-0-06-287260-9
18 19 20 21 22 SCP 10 9 8 7 6 5 4 3 2 1
❖
First Edition

Based on the Book Series by Kimberly and James Dean • Adapted by Anne Lamb from the Prime Video episode "Three Bite Rule" written by Josh Saltzman

Today's the potluck lunch at Pete's school, when everyone brings their favorite dish to share with the class.

Pete and Grumpy Toad are helping Mom make Pete's favorite dish, banana casserole. But Grumpy doesn't seem very excited.

"Are you really going to let people eat this?"
Grumpy asks.
Huh? Pete loves bananas!
"I don't like bananas." Grumpy shrugs.

"Have you ever tried a banana?"
asks Mom.

"I did," Grumpy says. "Once. It was
the worst taste-related day of my entire
life!"

"The flies were hovering around a
banana and my tongue accidentally
touched it!" Grumpy shudders at the
memory.

"Well, in this house we practice the Three Bite Rule," says Mom.

Grumpy looks confused, so Pete and Mom sing the Three Bite Rule song.

"To find out what you like, use this little tool.
Easy breezy as A-B-C, it's called the Three Bite Rule.
Now, you don't have to like it.
But you do have to try.
With just three teeny tiny bites, you might find something cool!

One bite . . .

two bite . . .

the Three Bite Rule!"

"The Three Bite Rule isn't only about food,"
says Mom. "It's also about trying anything and
everything, as long as you try it three times."

"Pete, you've never tried my pogo stick," says
Grumpy.

"Three Bite Rule!" everyone cheers.

So Pete bounces

one . . .

two . . .

three times on Grumpy's pogo stick.
Everyone claps for Pete.

"Wait a second," Grumpy says to Pete. "You said your mom won't try your skateboard!"

"Three Bite Rule!" everyone cheers again.

Mom gets on the skateboard and rolls once.

 "One . . ." she counts.

Mom rolls a second time. She's getting better!

 "Two . . ." says Mom.

Mom rolls a third time, but she's going very fast!

 "Threeeeeeeeeeeeeee!" Mom shouts.

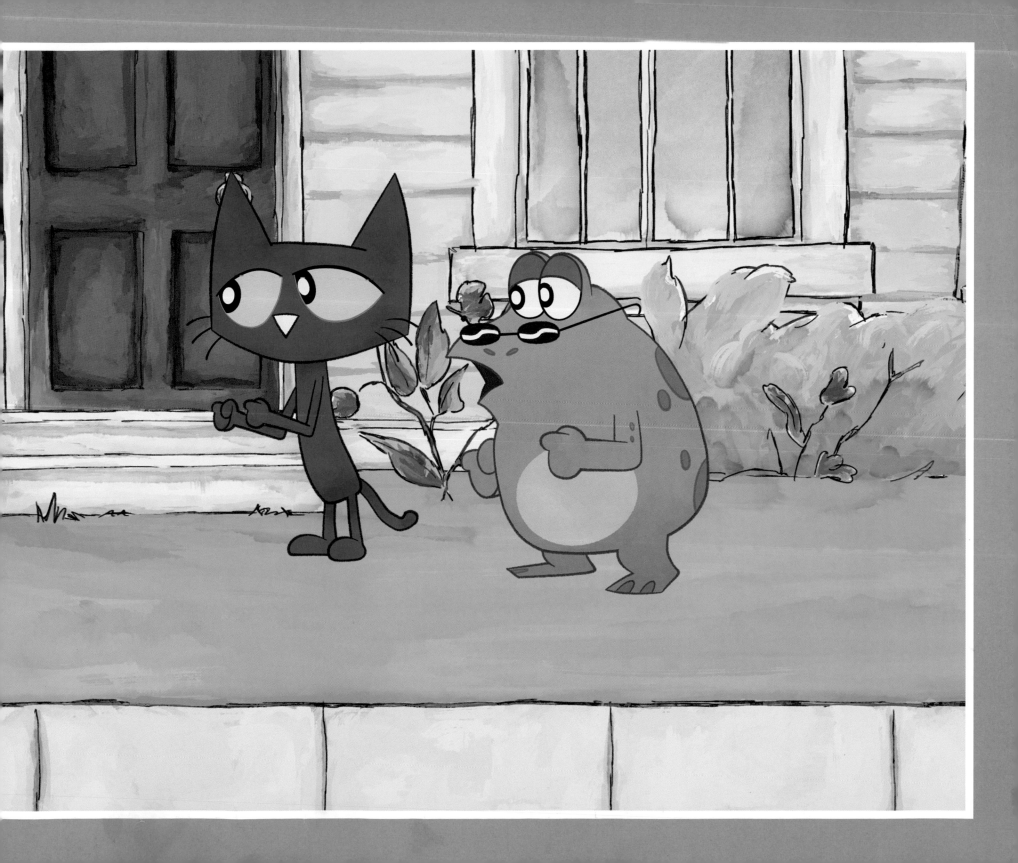

Grumpy smiles. "I REALLY like the Three Bite Rule!"
"Then why don't you find out if bananas are for you?"
asks Mom.
"Three Bite Rule!" Mom and Pete cheer.

Grumpy likes the Three Bite Rule when *other* people have to try new things. . . .

But he doesn't like it when *he* has to try new things.

Pete finds Grumpy outside.

"Nothing bad will happen if you just try a banana," Pete says.

"It's only three bites, right?" says Grumpy. "I think I'm ready for the Three Bite Rule."

It's finally time for the potluck lunch at school.

Dennis the Turtle brings slow-cooked cauliflower.

Callie brings scrambled egg burritos.

Emma brings fancy French toast.

Pete has never seen so many delicacies. He is very excited to Three Bite Rule everything on the table!

But Grumpy just snorts. "Potluck? More like
pot-BAD-luck."
   Seems like Grumpy has cold webbed feet
about the Three Bite Rule again.

Pete the Cat is there to give his friend that extra
pinch of courage.
   "Three Bite Rule! Three Bite Rule!" Pete sings to Grumpy.
   "Okay," Grumpy says. "Let's do this thing!"

So Grumpy tries his first bite of banana
casserole.
Everyone is watching.
"Hmmm," he says.

Grumpy eats a second bite.
"Okay . . ." he says.

Grumpy takes a third bite.
"Hey! I did it! I tried bananas!"

Everyone is waiting for Grumpy's reaction.

"Well, did you like them?" Callie finally asks.

"No! I didn't like them at all!" Grumpy laughs. "They tasted yucky! But that's okay! I'm okay, and now I know I don't like bananas because I tried them! I'm going to Three Bite Rule other things, too!"

So Grumpy tries three bites of Dennis's
slow-cooked cauliflower.
  "I'm a toad who likes cauliflower!" Grumpy
shouts.

Then Grumpy tries three bites of Callie's
scrambled egg burritos.
"Yum, yum, yum!" says Grumpy.

Then Grumpy tries three bites of Emma's fancy French toast.

"I think I like French toast even more than I like flies!" Grumpy says.

"You rocked the Three Bite Rule, Grumpy!" Emma says.

Everyone cheers for Grumpy. Pete is proud of his friend.

"I'm really glad I tried so many new things," Grumpy says. "Now it's your turn!"

Grumpy pulls out a plastic bag. Something inside it buzzes.

"Are those . . . ?" Callie starts to ask.

"That's right—flies!" Grumpy says. "Three Bite Rule!"

That's the Three Bite Rule! Try everything at least
three times . . . although maybe flies can be the
exception to the rule!